Mia and Nattie

One Great Team!

Written by
Marlene M. Bell

Illustrations by
Grace Sandford

For my husband, Gregg,
and for our sweet Natalie.

We miss you.
~ MMB

**Summary: A young girl helps a tiny lamb stay on the
farm by finding her a job.**

ISBN   979-8-9863409-1-3   (trade)

(1. Sheep—Fiction   2. Farming—Fiction)

First Edition

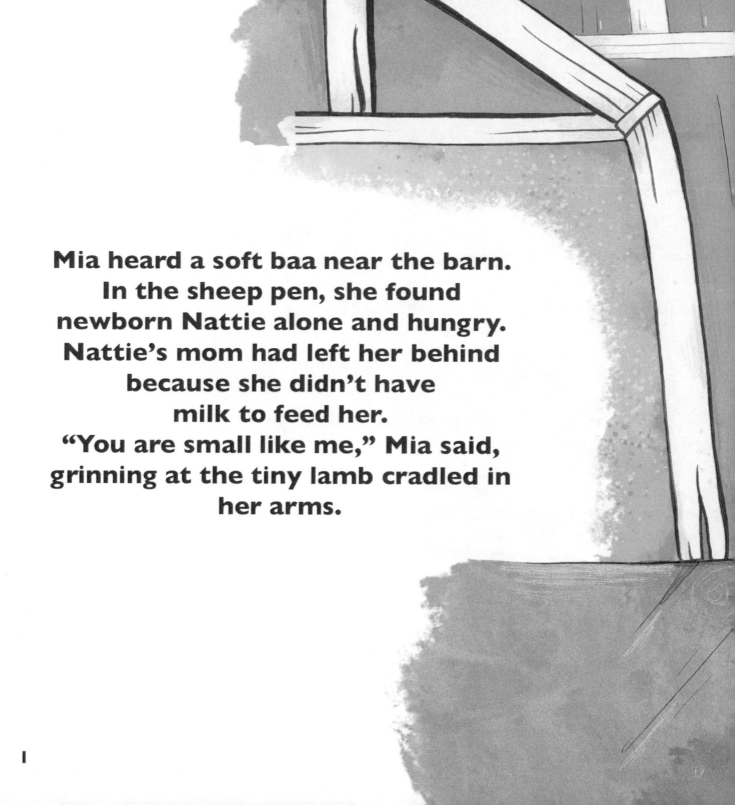

Mia heard a soft baa near the barn.
In the sheep pen, she found
newborn Nattie alone and hungry.
Nattie's mom had left her behind
because she didn't have
milk to feed her.
"You are small like me," Mia said,
grinning at the tiny lamb cradled in
her arms.

Mia brought Nattie into the laundry room to warm her.
"I hope Grandma will let me keep you inside," Mia said.
Nattie's mouth curved upward and she baaed in a weakened voi

Mia could see that Nattie's mouth was a little crooked.
And her legs were a bit shorter than usual, and one horn was
too straight like a unicorn's horn.

But Mia thought Nattie was perfect.

Nattie needed milk every few hours. Mia warmed her bottles and tried to be a good mama to the little sheep. But no matter how much Mia wished her lamb would grow, Nattie stayed small just like Mia.

In a hurry, Grandma nearly tripped over Nattie in the kitchen. Mia knew Nattie couldn't stay inside forever. But she hoped Grandma would give her some more time. She needed to help the little lamb get stronger. The day came when Grandma said, "Sheep belong outside."

Oh, no!

Mia wasn't ready.
She loved Nattie's calming manner. The
lamb made her feel special and tall,
instead of ordinary and small.

Mia knew what she had to do. She had
to teach Nattie how to live like the
other sheep.

Mia made Nattie a pen in the backyard,
and that afternoon, Nattie left the
laundry room for good.
Nattie cried for a while, but Mia stayed
with her until she felt comfortable in
her new home.

Mia changed Nattie's feeding plan as she grew.
She was no longer a baby lamb.
She was ready to learn how to become a grown ewe.

Tiny Nattie studied the ways of older sheep.
She ate grass and tasty weeds.
She ate grain and hay and drank water instead of milk.

But Nattie would never
be big enough to live with
the rest of the flock.
She was too small to raise
babies of her own.

"Your lamb needs a
home," Grandma
said to Mia.
"She has one! Please let
me keep her." Mia hugged
Nattie's neck.

Mia squinted back tears before they fell on Nattie's wool.
"A neighbor wants to buy her," Grandma said, then spun around and walked to the barn in silence.
Mia had to find a way for Nattie to stay.

While Mia thought, another sheep had her babies.
Mia found three lambs in the straw around lunchtime.
Two lambs had lots of room to get milk from their mom but they crowded out the smallest triplet brother.

"Grandma, one lamb needs more milk. Can we bottle feed him?" Mia asked.

Grandma hesitated a moment then picked up the weak lamb and said, "Maybe."

"He's small like Nattie, and she is alone. I will take him to her," Mia said.

14

The triplet grew fast with Mia feeding, and Nattie watching over him.
He soon joined his brothers and the rest of the sheep.
"Nattie is a terrific nanny," Mia said. She looked at Nattie and thought she caught her smiling.

"Nattie can't give us baby lambs. The neighbor's home is the best place for her," Grandma said.
"I know there is something Nattie can do on the farm," Mia answered.
Grandma turned away, shaking her head.

Mia had to come up with a plan.

Mia couldn't break Nattie's heart.

She wouldn't break Nattie's heart.

Mia watched Nattie rub her woolly body against a fence post. "Grandma, her wool itches. Can we shave it off?" Mia asked.
"No shearing today!" Grandma snapped. "My best ewe is sick."

"Put the sheep with Nattie. She helps me a lot when I'm sad," Mia said.
Grandma stayed quiet.
"Try it, please?" Mia pleaded. "Let her help."
Finally, Grandma shrugged. She walked to the barn to get the sheep.

A few minutes later, Grandma's tired sheep lay down in the grass. Nattie's mouth curved into a smile as she lay next to her.
"Nattie will work her magic. Just watch," Mia said.

Nattie's calming magic happened! Grandma's favorite sheep began to eat the grass. Mia laughed as Nattie and the sheep grazed on grass together.

"Well, look at that."
Grandma pointed
to the pair.
Nattie and the older ewe
jumped and
pranced about.
"I knew she would help."
Mia lifted her shoulders,
feeling ten feet tall.

Grandma winked at Mia.
"You were right, little one.
Nattie's handy to keep on the farm."
"Then you won't sell her?" Mia asked.
"Nattie is your sheep, forever," Grandma said.

Mia scratched Nattie's woolly ear and hugged her.
The two little friends made a good team.
Nattie snuggled close to Mia and gave her a
crooked smile.
Mia said, "Nattie, we will raise the orphans
together. Welcome to the farm."

Natalie plays peek-a-boo with Marlene.

Natalie's Story

Natalie the horned Dorset sheep defied nature with her strong will to live. I found her on a frosty morning during my 2 a.m. check for new babies at the barn. Natalie weighed just three pounds. Her mom had given birth too early and had no milk to feed her. I made the decision to take her inside, knowing that she would have a better chance of survival in the house, where I'd give her a warm water bath and a vigorous rub-down with a towel, then provide some saved mother's milk. For thirty years, the sheep we raised had lived outdoors, not inside our home. Until Natalie.

While the little lamb curled up on her towel in the laundry room, I worried. No lamb her size had survived more than a day, but Natalie was a fighter and proved me wrong at every turn. Natalie followed me to the kitchen every three hours while I made her milk. We would spend quiet time together where she worked wonders as my stress reliever. Natalie slowly gained weight and lived in the laundry room for weeks until she made such a mess that I had no choice but to move her outside. In the backyard, Natalie continued to grow, but not enough to live with the other sheep, so she grazed on grass nearby and became our "Nattie" with a goofy horn and a crooked mouth.

Even though Nattie was doing quite well, I still worried, because sheep are flocking animals. They need other sheep to be happy. One September, a newly orphaned lamb needed milk. He would grow better with a buddy, and I couldn't imagine a more ideal buddy than Nattie. Soon, she took over as a nanny for all of our bottle lambs each spring and fall. Nattie roamed our farm for thirteen years, providing companionship to orphaned lambs and aging sheep. Her job on the ranch was just as important as mine.

Mia and Nattie is **N**atalie's story.

Made in the USA
Middletown, DE
16 April 2023

28973095R00020